Grandma's
BROWN CHAIR

by Nancy Wiedmeyer

Illustrations by Annette Schuh

MINDSTIR MEDIA

Published by Mindstir Media, LLC
1931 Woodbury Ave. #182 | Portsmouth, New Hampshire 03801 | USA
1.800.767.0531 | www.mindstirmedia.com

Printed in the United States of America
ISBN-13: 978-0-9972233-0-9
Library of Congress Control Number: 2016900815

This book is dedicated to our children:
Catherine, Julie, Nathan, Connie, Ryan, Owen and Neil

This is Grandma's brown chair.
It sits in her living room along the wall not far from the TV.
Everyone in my family loves to sit in Grandma's brown chair.
It is wide and deep, close to the floor, and velvety soft.

I scraped my knees when I fell off my bike and ran into the house crying. Grandma snuggled with me in her brown chair. She kissed my head and softly hummed, "Twinkle, twinkle little star". My knees felt much better.

I was mad and cried when my sister teased me and called me a big baby. Mama held me on her lap in Grandma's brown chair. She rubbed my head and hummed a song in my ear. I didn't care that my sister called me a baby anymore.

My sister and I scrunch close together in Grandma's brown chair while we watch a scary show on TV.
We don't feel so scared then.

After work, my Dad can slouch down and fall asleep in Grandma's brown chair. We don't mind, except when he snores.
If I shake his foot, he stops.

When I'm sleepy, I curl up with my blanket
in Grandma's brown chair.

Whiskers, my old cat, tries to get Grandma's brown chair
to herself whenever she can.
But she doesn't mind if she has to share.

Sometimes I find surprises in
Grandma's brown chair.
I found a red whistle and
some green M&M's.
Once I even found a quarter.

Even my brother with his six-foot-long legs, hangs them over Grandma's brown chair and listens to his music.

My dog, Willie, curls himself around Grandma's brown chair
and doesn't care who wants to sit in it, it's his.

The only one who does not like Grandma's brown chair, is...

Grandpa! He sits in his own green chair.

Printed in the USA
CPSIA information can be obtained
at www.ICGtesting.com
LVHW071919191023
761567LV00011B/39